SUPER HEROES

AND THE FALSE DESTINY

WRITTEN BY
MICHAEL ANTHONY STEELE

ILLUSTRATED BY
LEONEL CASTELLANI

STONE ARCH BOOKS
a capstone imprint

Published by Stone Arch Books,
an imprint of Capstone.
1710 Roe Crest Drive
North Mankato, Minnesota 56003
www.capstonepub.com

Library of Congress Cataloging-in-Publication Data
is available on the Library of Congress website.
ISBN: 978-1-4965-8722-0 (library binding)
ISBN: 978-1-4965-9200-2 (paperback)
ISBN: 978-1-4965-8726-8 (eBook PDF)

Summary: When Batman introduces a new Justice League
hopeful, Green Arrow gets suspicious. Who is this new hero and why
should they trust him? But his questions are quickly pushed aside when
members of the Justice League suddenly start losing their powers. Little
do they know, a super-villain in their midst has set his sights on
the team's Watchtower satellite. Can the Justice League save their
headquarters before it's too late?

Designer: Kyle Grenz

Printed and bound in the USA.
PA100

TABLE OF CONTENTS

When the champions of Earth came together to battle a threat too big for a single hero, they realized the value of strength in numbers. Together they formed an unstoppable team, dedicated to defending the planet from the forces of evil.

They are the . . .

JUSTICE LEAGUE™

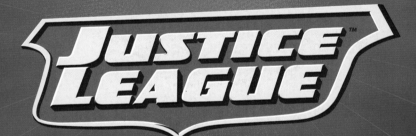

CHAPTER 1

A NEW HERO

VRRRRRRROOOOM!!!

Five motorcycles zoomed through the busy streets of Central City. The riders zipped around cars and raced over sidewalks as they chased their target. Citizens screamed and leaped out of the way as the motorcycles roared by.

The rider on the lead cycle pointed up toward a nearby building. "There he is!"

"Don't let him get away," a second rider shouted over the roar of the cycles.

A dark figure ran along a ledge above them. Keeping to the shadows, he jumped toward another building, flying across the night sky. The man grabbed onto a drainpipe at the last second and slid down to the ground. He then disappeared between two buildings.

"We have him now!" the lead rider said as he turned his bike into the alley.

The other riders followed. Their roaring motors echoed off the buildings as they zoomed toward the running man.

The man reached a dead end and spun around to face his pursuers. He stepped into the light and reached up to adjust his hat. It was Green Arrow.

The motorcycles spread out before coming to a stop. The riders climbed off their bikes and removed their helmets.

"I'm sick and tired of you meddling in our territory," the leader said. He glanced at the other street thugs blocking the way they had come. They pulled out pipes and chains. "It's time to teach you a lesson. And there's no way out."

Green Arrow raised an index finger. "Hold that thought."

The super hero pulled an arrow from his quiver and loaded his bow in one smooth motion. He shot the arrow past the thugs, and it struck the bottom of a stack of metal barrels. The barrels tipped to one side and rattled as they fell over and blocked the alleyway.

Green Arrow grinned. "*Now* there's no way out."

"Get him!" ordered the leader.

The five criminals moved in. Green Arrow ducked as one thug swung a pipe. Then he leaped out of the way as another threw a reckless punch.

WHACK!

The super hero swung his bow, knocking both of them back.

Another crook whipped his chain and wrapped it around Green Arrow's bow. The hero pulled with all his might, jerking the criminal off his feet. He went flying toward the other thugs, knocking two to the ground.

"All right," Green Arrow said. "Enough playing around." He pulled an arrow from his quiver and shot it straight up.

"What was that for?" asked the leader as they closed in again.

Green Arrow shrugged. "You'll see."

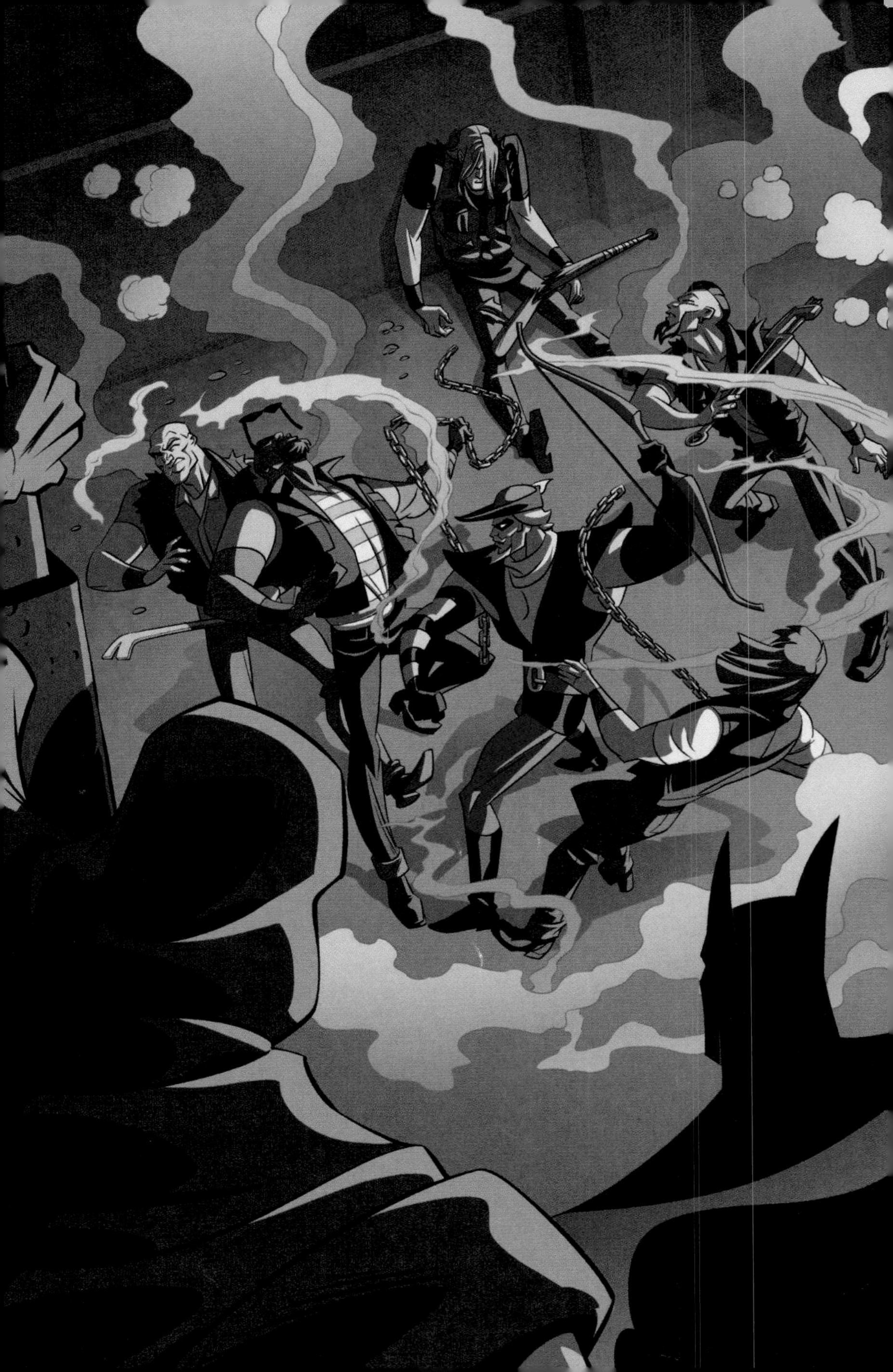

The arrow sped back down, landing in the middle of the group of thugs. It exploded into a cloud of smoke, swallowing them all.

While the crooks were distracted, the super hero made his move. He leaped into the cloud and took out the thugs with several well-placed punches, kicks, and swings of his bow. When the smoke finally cleared, Green Arrow was the only one standing.

He dusted off his hands. "I must be out of practice. That took longer than I expected."

The hero crouched down and placed handcuffs on one of the criminals. But he didn't notice the leader waking up. The crook stumbled over to his motorcycle and climbed on. Green Arrow was facing away from the bike when it started up and raced toward him. The crook smiled as he aimed for the unsuspecting hero.

ZZZZZZP!

Something shot out of the night and struck the motorcycle's front tire. The tire stopped instantly, but the rest of the bike didn't. It flipped up and over, flying above the crouched hero. The rider screamed as both he and his bike crashed into a mound of garbage bags at the end of the alley.

Green Arrow reached down and picked up the object that had struck the tire. It was one of Batman's Batarangs.

"You know, I was wondering if you were going to lend a hand," Green Arrow said. "Or just sit up there and watch the show."

A caped figure dropped to the ground—it was Batman.

"And who's your friend?" Green Arrow asked.

Another figure landed beside Batman. He wore a blue costume with a gray cape and hood. A gray mask covered his entire face.

"This is Gray Hood," Batman said. "He's trying out to be a member of the Justice League."

The man in the gray hood nodded a greeting.

"I brought him here to watch you work," Batman explained. "He's like us. No superpowers, using skill alone to fight crime."

"Well, if Batman trusts you, then I trust you," Green Arrow said. He leaned forward and smirked. "Because Batman here doesn't trust anyone."

"Gray Hood is highly skilled at guessing his foe's next move," Batman continued.

"Oh yeah?" Green Arrow asked.

The archer whipped out an arrow with a boxing glove on the tip. He shot it at the new super hero with lightning speed. Gray Hood leaned to one side, easily dodging it.

"Not bad," Green Arrow said.

Green Arrow took a step forward and swung his bow at Gray Hood. The new hero dodged one swing, and another, then another. His gray cape swirled as he dropped to the ground and swung a leg under Green Arrow. The archer's legs flew out from under him, and he plopped to the ground.

"Told you," said Batman with a slight smile.

Gray Hood stood and held a hand out to the fallen hero. Green Arrow laughed as he took his outstretched hand and got to his feet.

"Nice moves," Green Arrow said.

Gray Hood simply nodded again.

"You don't say much, do you?" asked Green Arrow.

Suddenly, sirens filled the night air. Batman held a hand to the side of his head as he listened to the police radio.

"Major apartment fire," the Dark Knight announced. He pulled the grapnel from his Utility Belt and fired it toward a nearby building. He pressed a button, and the device hauled him off the ground and into the air.

WHOOSH!

Gray Hood fired a similar tool and was right behind him. Green Arrow grabbed one of the crooks' motorcycles and hit the gas. He jumped over the pile of barrels and sped after the two heroes.

The burning high-rise building was just a block away, so all three super heroes arrived in the nick of time. But that didn't really matter, because another Justice League member was on the scene—The Flash.

The front door of the building glowed with a blur of red and yellow. The speeding super hero carried every resident out of the door in the blink of an eye. When everyone was a safe distance away, he skidded to a stop in front of Batman, Green Arrow, and Gray Hood.

"That's everyone," said The Flash. "Now I'll put out the fire."

The speedster ran around the high-rise in a big circle. He ran so fast that he created a mini tornado. The spiraling winds sucked the air out of the building and snuffed out the flames inside.

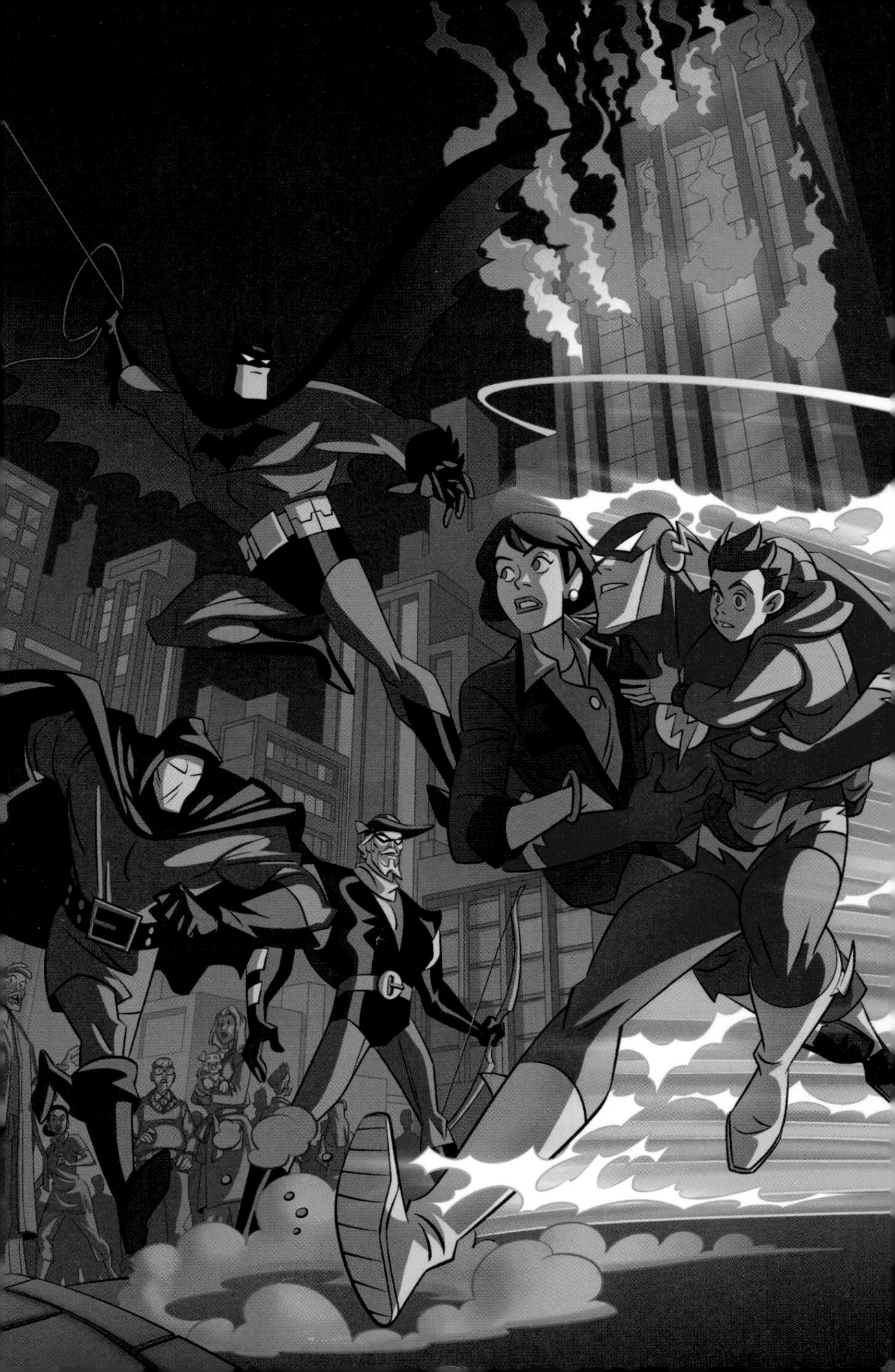

The Flash was a blur as he poured on the speed until he ran on the walls themselves. He ran up the building, forcing the tornado higher and higher. Soon, the last of the flames flickered above the high-rise. With no more air, they simply faded to nothingness.

The Flash began to speed back down the building, but something went wrong. He slowed down so much that he no longer ran along the outside. His arms and legs flailed as he began to fall.

"He's in trouble," Batman said. He fired his grapnel at the building.

Green Arrow loaded a special arrow and shot it toward the falling hero. As the arrow neared The Flash, it exploded into a wide net. The net wrapped around the hero, snaring him in a big rope ball.

Batman swung in and caught the netting with one hand. He carefully lowered the hero to the ground.

"What happened, Flash?" asked Green Arrow.

"I don't know," the Scarlet Speedster replied. "I . . . I just lost my speed."

CHAPTER 2

LOSS OF POWER

The Watchtower was the Justice League's home base. It was a large satellite that orbited Earth. Its training room had fighting robots the heroes could use for practice. Green Arrow decided to get in a workout while Cyborg checked out The Flash.

The hero loaded three arrows at once and fired. The arrows flew across the room and struck three different attacking robots. Sparks danced over their metal bodies, and they crumpled to the ground. But five other robots kept coming.

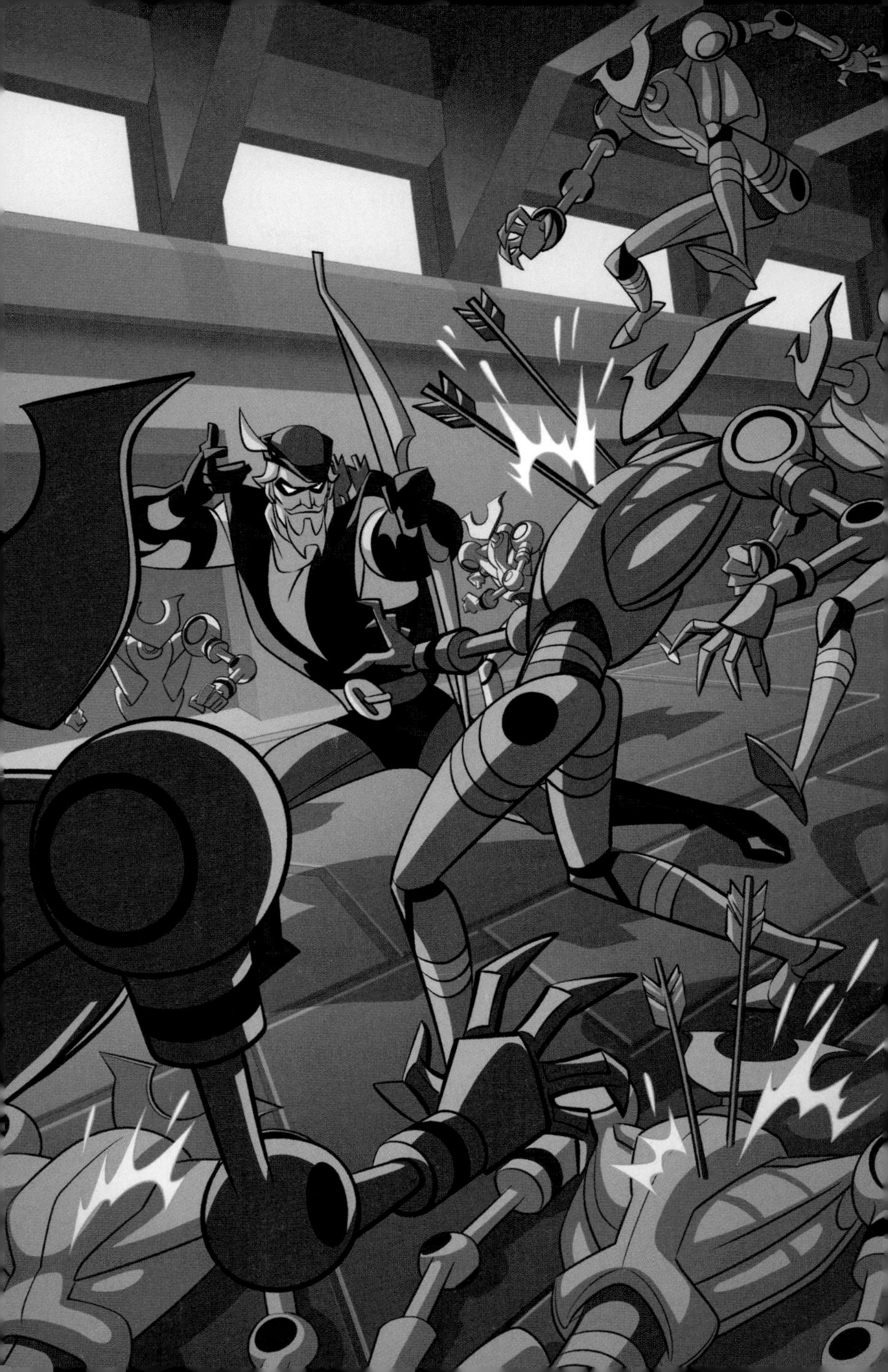

Three robots ran straight at the hero, while two of them split off from the others. Green Arrow swung his bow, knocking one robot back. He ducked as the other two robots threw punches. They ended up hitting each other instead.

The last two robots crawled along the walls, trying to sneak up on the hero. With amazing speed, Green Arrow loaded another arrow and fired. He pinned one robot to the wall before it could attack.

The other robot leaped off the wall and landed on the hero's back. Green Arrow grabbed its arm and tossed it over his shoulder. When it landed on the ground, the hero slammed a foot on its chest.

SIZZZZLE!

Sparks burst from the robot's body as it shut down.

"It's a good thing Cyborg created these robots to repair themselves," Wonder Woman said as she stepped into the training room. "Otherwise no one else would get a turn."

The robots were already getting to their feet. Some removed the arrows and handed them back to the hero.

"Ah, I got sick of waiting around," Green Arrow said. "How's The Flash doing?"

"I was on my way to check," Wonder Woman said. "Why don't you join me?"

The two heroes left the training room and marched toward the medical bay. There they found Batman and Gray Hood standing outside a large viewing window.

Through the window, The Flash lay on an exam table while Cyborg checked the readings on a nearby computer screen.

"Any news?" asked Wonder Woman.

Cyborg shook his head. "I've run test after test, and I can't find anything wrong with him." He pointed to the screen. "The Flash is in perfect health."

"I don't know what it is," said The Flash. "I completely lost my connection to the Speed Force." The Speed Force was the cosmic force that gave The Flash his powers.

Green Arrow turned to Gray Hood. "Any thoughts, new guy?"

Gray Hood simply shrugged.

Green Arrow held up both hands. "Whoa, hey, don't talk my ear off."

Suddenly, red light filled the hallway. Cyborg tilted his head. "I'm getting an alert." Part man, part robot, the hero was tied in to the Watchtower's computer system.

"There's a major volcanic eruption in Italy," he reported. "The people there may need our help."

"You stay with The Flash," Batman said. "We can handle it."

Green Arrow nudged Gray Hood. "Italy's great this time of year, huh?"

The new super hero didn't respond.

"Nothing, huh?" asked Green Arrow. "Sheesh, and I thought Batman was the dark and brooding type."

Batman, Wonder Woman, Green Arrow, and Gray Hood boarded the Justice League's jet called the Javelin and flew back to Earth. They rocketed to Italy and landed just outside a small coastal village. The nearby volcano spewed smoke, ash, and hot lava as villagers ran for their lives.

The heroes exited the jet and sprang into action. Wonder Woman picked up a bus and flew it toward the center of town. Green Arrow, Batman, and Gray Hood ushered people onto the bus while Wonder Woman gathered more vehicles.

"We could really use The Flash right now to check all the buildings," Green Arrow said.

"We'll have to do it ourselves," Batman replied. "Spread out and look for survivors."

The heroes searched every home and got more villagers into more waiting vehicles. As the buses and trucks drove away, Wonder Woman flew into the air to get a better look. A river of lava rushed toward the town. It burned up everything in its path. A few people still ran from the destruction.

"I'm afraid we're not going to make it," she said.

"I can buy you more time," said a nearby voice. It was John Stewart, the Green Lantern.

The hero landed beside the village and aimed his ring at the volcano. In a flash of green light, his ring formed a long wall. It blocked the flow of lava and directed it to the nearby coast. Instead of burning the homes, the lava flowed into the ocean. *TSSSSSSSS!* Steam billowed out of the water.

"Go, Team Green!" shouted Green Arrow. He snatched up a small goat and handed it to a fleeing farmer.

With Green Lantern holding back the destructive lava flow, the rest of the heroes got everyone to safety.

Suddenly, Green Lantern grunted in pain. "Something's . . . wrong," he said as he grabbed his wrist and concentrated. "I . . . I can't hold it!"

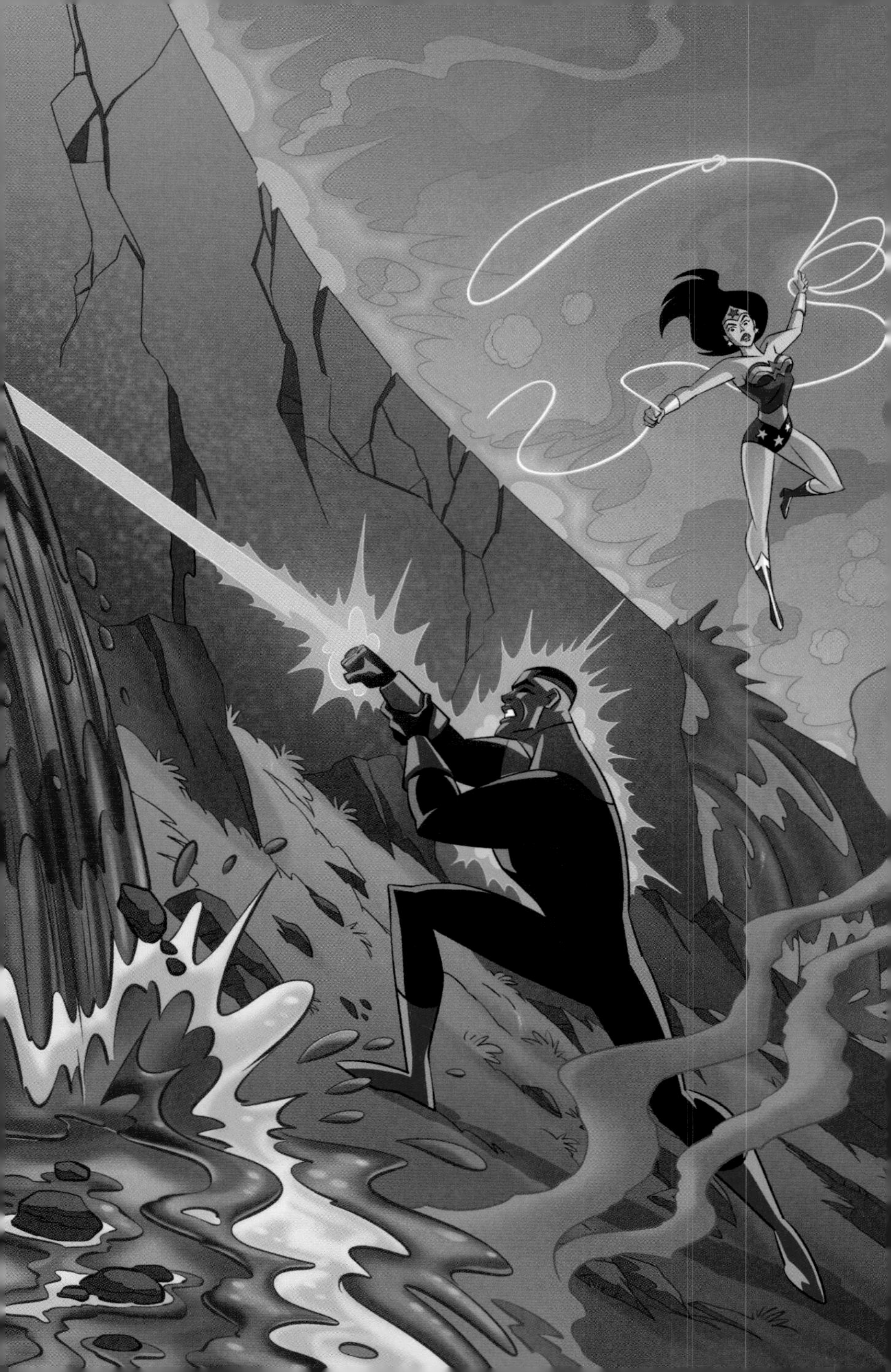

The large green wall flickered and began to crumble. The lava splashed through holes in the wall like a tidal wave. Green Lantern shook his ring and concentrated, trying to bring the wall back.

Wonder Woman flew down and lassoed Green Lantern with her golden rope. She snatched him away from the lava in the nick of time.

"I don't know what happened," Green Lantern said as he dangled in the air. "I can't seem to concentrate."

"Don't worry, John," Wonder Woman said as she hauled him to safety. "You bought us enough time to save everyone."

As the two neared the others waiting at the Javelin, Wonder Woman struggled to stay in the sky.

"I feel . . . so weak," the Amazon Princess said. Suddenly, she dropped Green Lantern and then fell to the ground beside him.

The other heroes ran up to them. "What happened out there?" asked Batman.

Green Lantern stumbled to his feet. "I don't know," he said.

Wonder Woman could barely stand. "It's as if . . . I'm powerless."

CHAPTER 3

NO HOLDING BACK

Wonder Woman and Green Lantern lay on exam tables next to The Flash. Cyborg moved from one screen to the next, trying to find anything that would have taken away their powers.

"It doesn't make any sense," Cyborg said. "Each one of them is completely healthy."

"Is it some kind of virus?" Green Arrow asked. He and Gray Hood looked in through the viewing window.

"That's the first thing I checked," Cyborg replied. "I'm adjusting my sensors in case it's an alien virus we've never seen before." He turned to another screen as data streamed across it at incredible speeds. "But so far, it's just affecting those with superpowers or a connection to a power source—like the Speed Force or a power ring."

Green Arrow nudged Gray Hood in the arm. "I never thought I'd be glad not to have special powers, huh?"

The new super hero just nodded.

"Ah, come on," Green Arrow said. "You gotta give me something."

Green Arrow threw up his hands and headed for the control deck. Gray Hood followed as they found Batman working in the Watchtower's control center. The Dark Knight studied the many computer screens.

"Any luck on your end, Batman?" Green Arrow asked.

"I haven't been able to find anything connecting our last two locations," the Dark Knight reported. "No strange radiation, no meteor strikes . . . nothing."

Green Arrow glanced over at Gray Hood. The new super hero had been at both locations.

Could he be the cause of it somehow? Green Arrow thought.

Green Arrow opened his mouth to speak when a small red light blinked on the console. Batman pressed a button, and a city map filled the screen. His lips tightened as he recognized the image.

"This will have to wait for now," Batman said. "There's trouble in Gotham City."

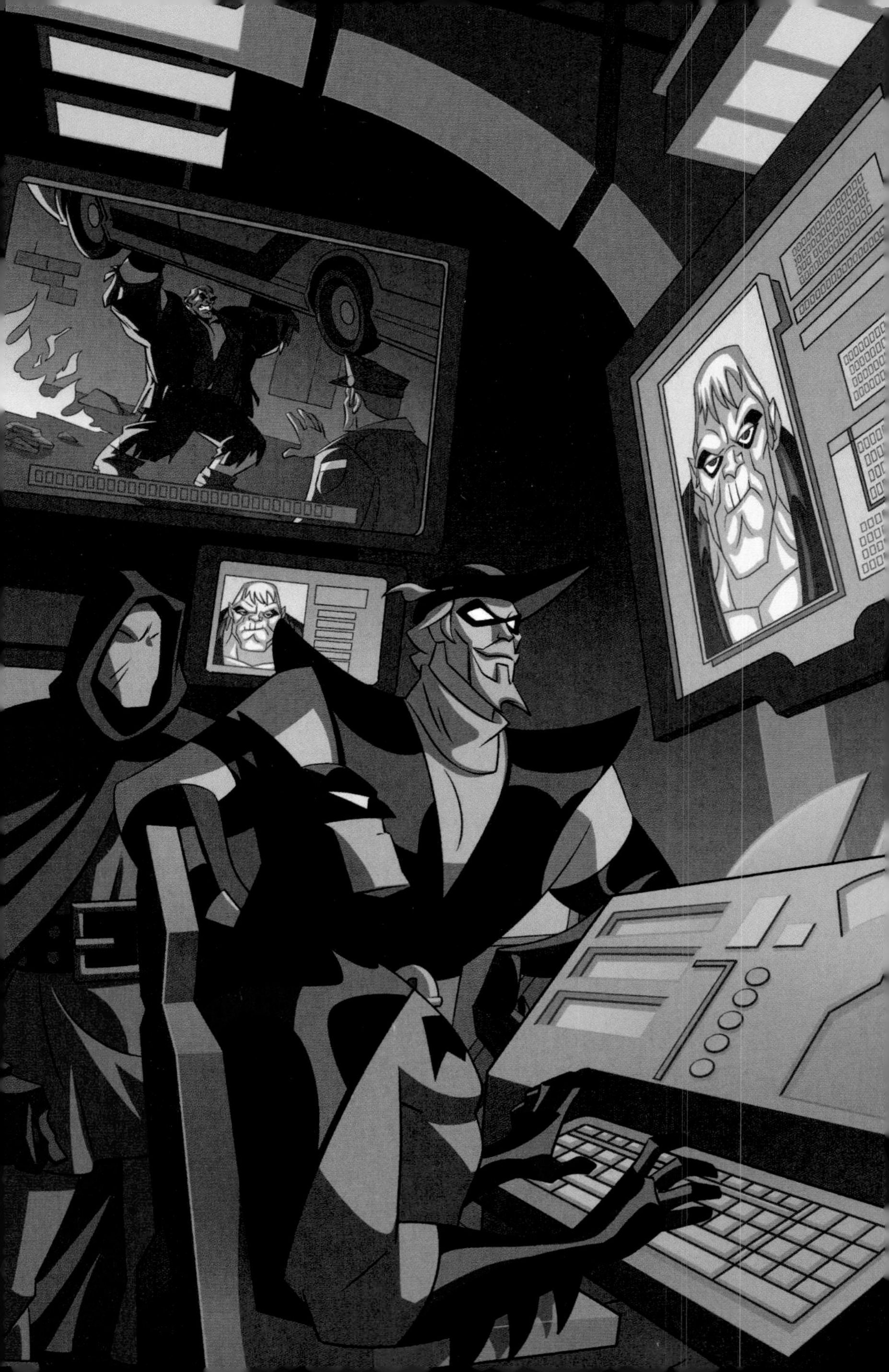

Batman's fingers flew over the keyboard, and a video filled one of the screens. A giant pale figure in tattered clothing raised a police car over his head. Officers scattered as the monster hurled the squad car toward them.

"Solomon Grundy has broken out of Blackgate Prison," Batman said.

Green Arrow tightened his grip on his bow. "Then what are we waiting for?"

The three heroes boarded the Javelin and rocketed toward Gotham City. When the sleek jet reached the city, it soared over the surrounding police cars and landed in the large parking lot of an abandoned building. The heroes exited the plane to find Solomon Grundy cornered against the building.

"Grundy no go back!" bellowed the giant. "Grundy smash anyone who tries to make him go!"

"Solomon Grundy is an undead monster with super-strength," Batman explained. "No need to hold back."

Gray Hood ran straight for the giant. Grundy punched at the hero with huge fists, but Gray Hood easily dodged the mighty blows. Instead of throwing his own punch, the hero grabbed Grundy's arm and flipped him over his shoulder.

BAM! The beast slammed into a nearby dumpster. He growled as he climbed out of the crumpled metal.

"Watch and learn, new guy," Green Arrow said. He loaded four arrows and fired them at once.

As the arrows neared the villain, they spread out, revealing a large net between them. The net scooped up the giant and pinned him against a brick wall.

Green Arrow grinned as the beast grunted and struggled to break free. "That wasn't so hard," the hero said.

Grundy growled as he finally tore through the netting.

"You'll need something stronger than that for Grundy," Batman said.

"What do you think about this?" Green Arrow asked as he pulled another arrow from his quiver. He fired it square at the villain's chest.

KA-THOOM! The arrow exploded, and fire and smoke swallowed the giant.

"I think you just made him angry," Batman replied.

When the smoke cleared, Solomon Grundy balled his hands into fists and roared with rage.

Batman ran straight for the giant. He darted to one side when Grundy brought down a stomping foot. He ducked as Grundy punched at him with a huge fist. The Dark Knight ran up the villain's chest and then back-flipped into the air.

Grundy tried to grab him but was too late. Instead, the giant looked confused as several bat-shaped explosives now covered his body. Their red lights blinked faster as Grundy tried to brush them off.

BAM·BA·BAM·BAM·BA·BAM·BAM!

The explosives rippled across Grundy's body. Smoke and flames filled the air as the monster stumbled backward. When the smoke cleared, Solomon Grundy shook his head—dizzy but still awake.

"Now Grundy really mad!" the beast shouted.

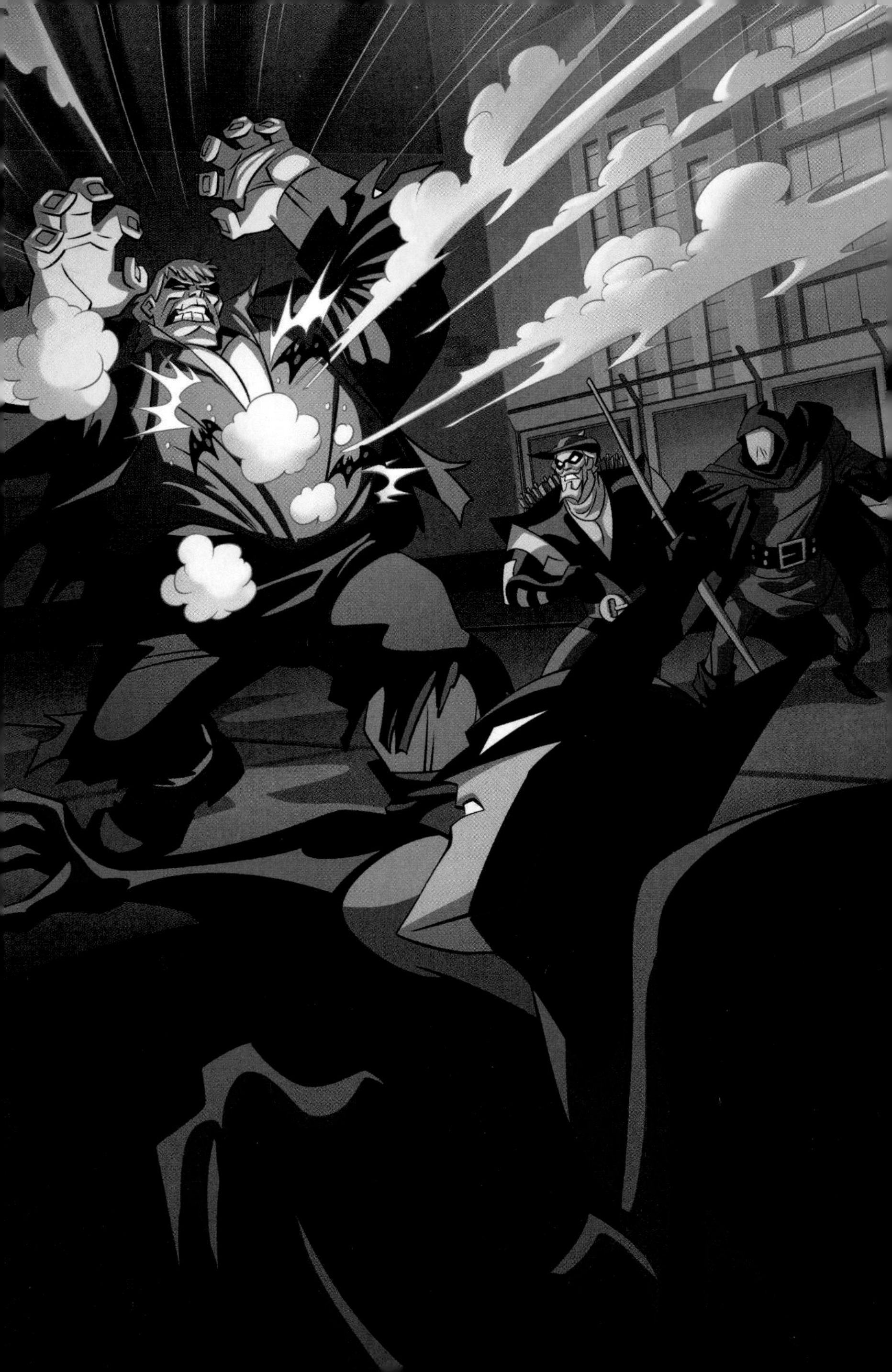

"What's going to take this guy down?" Green Arrow asked.

A streak of red and blue zipped down from the sky and rocketed toward Grundy. *POW!* It struck the monster and pushed him back toward the abandoned building.

KA-BAM!

Bricks flew everywhere as the giant slammed into the wall.

The dust settled, revealing Superman pinning the monster inside a hole in the brick wall.

Grundy groggily tried to fight back but was too slow. The Man of Steel pounded the villain with blow after blow.

POW-POW-POP-POP-POP-POW!

Solomon Grundy finally stopped moving. He was out cold.

Superman floated away from the unconscious villain. "Cyborg told me you were a little shorthanded," he said. "Thought I'd swing by and lend a hand."

Green Arrow nodded at Grundy. "Looks like you lent several."

Batman pointed past the Man of Steel. "Superman, the building!"

A crack formed in the bricks. It began at the hole and raced up the side of the building. One side of the three-story building began to fall away.

WHOOSH!

Superman flew up and easily caught the wall and pushed it back. He almost had it back in place when sweat formed on his brow. He groaned as he suddenly struggled with the load.

"Don't . . . understand," Superman grunted. "This should be . . . easy."

"Superman?" Green Arrow asked.

WHAM! The wall slammed to the ground on top of the Man of Steel.

"Superman!" Green Arrow shouted.

The three heroes ran over to what was now just a pile of rubble. They quickly pulled away brick after brick until they uncovered Superman. The super hero was unhurt, just trapped under the heavy load.

"I . . . I don't know what happened," Superman said as he stumbled out of the pile. "Suddenly, all my strength was just . . . gone."

CHAPTER 4

A NEW REALITY

Green Arrow paced back and forth outside the medical bay's window. Superman now lay on a table next to the other weakened heroes. While Green Arrow paced, Batman stood silently, staring at his teammates.

"This doesn't make any sense," Green Arrow said. "Cyborg can't find anything wrong with them. You can't find any connection. This is crazy."

"I know," Batman said.

"What about this Gray Hood guy?" Green Arrow asked. "You know, this didn't start happening until he showed up."

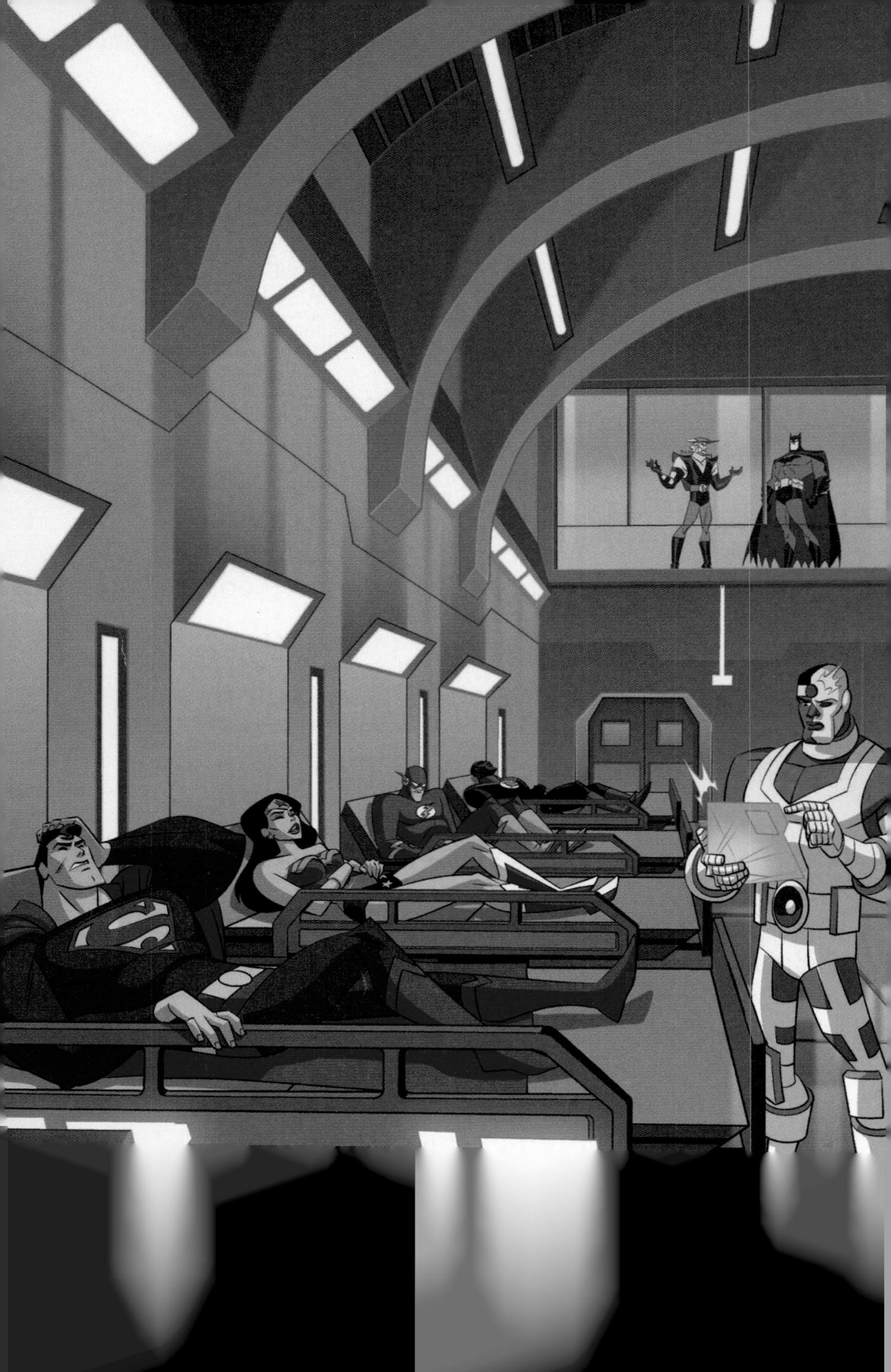

"Gray Hood is not the problem," Batman said. "I trust him."

"Oh yeah?" Green Arrow stopped pacing. "Why is that? Why do you trust him?"

"I just do," replied the Dark Knight.

"Yeah, but *why?*" Green Arrow repeated. "You don't trust anybody."

Batman cocked his head. "I . . . I don't really know."

"Does that make any sense?" asked Green Arrow. "You're the World's Greatest Detective. You must have a logical reason to trust him."

"You're right, I should—but I don't," Batman grabbed his head and winced in pain. "It's as if something in my mind is ordering me to trust him."

Green Arrow glanced around. "Where is he now?"

"In the command center," Batman replied. "Cyborg put him in charge of the Watchtower."

"What?!!" Green Arrow threw up his hands. "Gray Hood's not even a member of the league yet. That doesn't make sense!"

Batman's lips tightened. "No, it doesn't."

The two heroes ran for the elevator and headed for the command deck. When they exited the elevator, Green Arrow took the lead as they sprinted down the corridor. The heroes skidded to a stop in front of the door leading to the command center. Green Arrow reached for the access button.

"Something's wrong," Batman said, glancing around. His eyes widened. "Wait!"

It was too late. Green Arrow pressed the button, and the doors slid open.

WHOOOOOSH!

A gust of wind filled the corridor as the air was sucked out of the space station. The two heroes were swept toward the doorway and the vacuum of space.

Before the rushing air could sweep them out, a hook on a rope shot across the room. **ZZ-KLANK!** It latched onto the opposite wall.

The Dark Knight held tight to the grapnel with one hand. His other hand gripped a green bow. Green Arrow clutched at the other end of the bow.

As Batman reeled them in, Green Arrow grabbed an arrow from his quiver. Stretching as far as he could reach, he used its tip to hit the access button. The doors slid shut, and the heroes dropped to the floor. The command center door shimmered. Then it changed into its true form. It was really the air-lock door.

Green Arrow stumbled to his feet. "How did you know something was wrong?"

The Dark Knight took in deep breaths. "The command center entrance is forty-three steps from the elevator," he replied. "We had only gone twenty-four."

"You know how many steps there are to the command center?" asked Green Arrow.

"I pay attention," Batman replied. "But the important thing is that someone is playing with the way we see reality."

HA! HA! HA! HA! HA! Laughter echoed through the corridor.

Suddenly every view screen in the hallway flickered to life. An image of Gray Hood appeared on every one.

"Very good, Batman," said Gray Hood. "You just found a major piece of the puzzle."

"Hey, you *can* talk," said Green Arrow.

"Oh, I can do much more than that," Hood told him. "Isn't that right, Batman?"

The Dark Knight scowled. "I think so. ESP, mind control, turning dreams into nightmares." He turned to Green Arrow. "I believe Gray Hood is actually a criminal named John Dee."

"You know I prefer my true name." The villain's gray mask faded away to reveal the face of a grinning skull. "Doctor Destiny."

"Whoa." Green Arrow raised his eyebrows. "The dream guy?"

Doctor Destiny roared with laughter. "Not so simple," he said. "I'm also the . . . *guy* who plants suggestions into people's minds telling them to trust me, to give me complete control of the Watchtower . . ."

"Or convincing them they've lost their superpowers," Batman continued.

Destiny raised a hand. "Guilty as charged."

Green Arrow pulled an arrow from his quiver and loaded his bow. "Then it's a good thing neither of us has superpowers."

"Did you not hear the part about having complete control of this station?" Destiny asked. "I can take care of you two with just a press of a button."

A door at the end of the corridor slid open. Out marched dozens of training robots. Their metal feet clanked on the floor as they charged toward the heroes.

HA! HA! HA! HA! HA! Doctor Destiny's laughter filled the air.

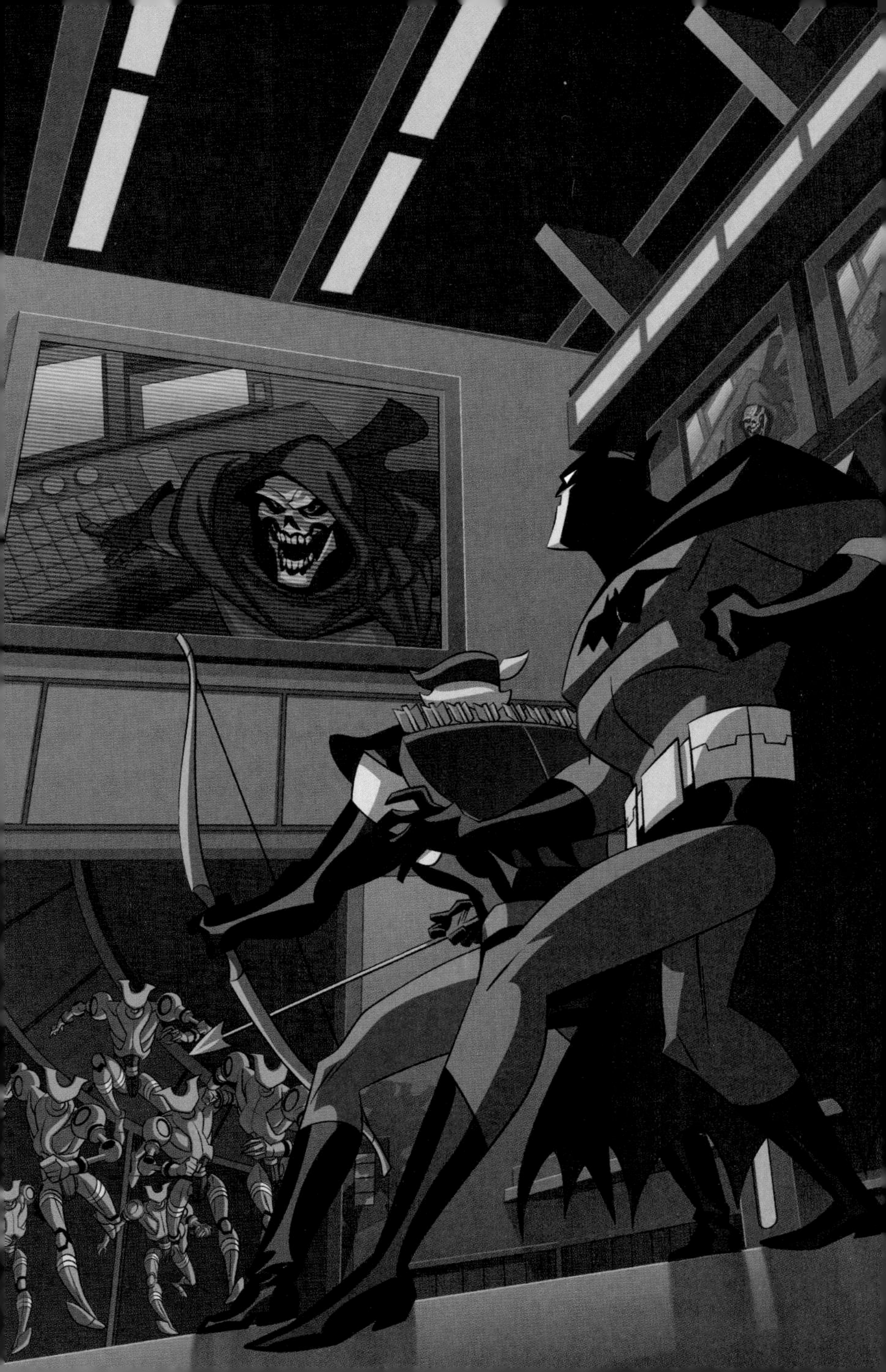

CHAPTER 5

A NEAR MISS

POW! KA-POW!

Two explosive arrows hit their targets. They blasted two of the training robots to pieces. Unfortunately, as Green Arrow pulled another arrow from his quiver, the pieces were already re-forming. The robots were repairing themselves.

Batman fought off five robots at once. He punched one in the chest and flipped another one, slamming it to the ground. A spinning kick sent another robot hurtling backward, crashing into two more.

Each robot went down in a shower of sparks. Each robot also began to repair itself. One by one, they stood and got in line behind others, preparing to rejoin the battle.

"This fight is endless," Green Arrow said as he swung his bow. A robot's arm flew down the corridor. "We need to get the others. Let them know that this power business is all in their minds."

"There's no time," Batman said as he kicked off another robot. "If Doctor Destiny has complete control of the Watchtower, there's no telling what damage he can cause." The Dark Knight sent Batarangs flying. They slammed into robots, taking them out temporarily.

"Besides, his mind control is too powerful," Batman continued. "We have to take out Destiny ourselves."

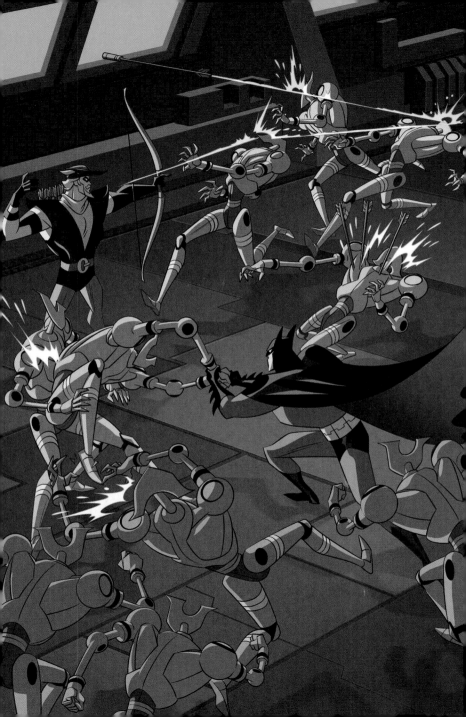

"How can we do that if we can't even get in the control room?" Green Arrow asked. He shot an arrow that bounced off the heads of three robots.

"We create a different reality of our own," Batman said. He tossed a robot over his head. It crashed into four more. "Come on!"

Batman ran down the corridor with Green Arrow close behind. The mass of training robots charged after them. The two heroes slowly pulled ahead, getting more space between them and the robots.

When they had a big enough lead, they turned a sharp corner. Batman opened a storage closet and darted inside. Green Arrow followed and closed the door behind him.

"Now what?" Green Arrow whispered. The sound of marching metal feet echoed on the other side of the door.

"How are you at reprogramming training robots?" Batman asked. The metal footsteps faded into silence.

Green Arrow grinned. "Just get me one and I'll show you."

"I'll get you two," Batman said as he slid open the door. He glanced outside and then disappeared through the open doorway.

There were sounds of a struggle. Batman grunted, metal clanked, and then all was silent. Green Arrow was about to lean out the door when the heads of two robots came into view. Green Arrow started to swing his bow when he saw that Batman held the robots from behind. The door slid shut behind him as he dropped the sparking robots to the floor. Green Arrow went to work on them before they repaired themselves.

* * *

Doctor Destiny laughed as he watched the video on one of the view screens. It was from a camera in the medical lab. It showed Cyborg checking over his patients on the exam tables. The hero looked baffled as he went over the data on the screens.

"Poor Cyborg," Destiny said. "In your mind, you're so close to the solution and then it just . . . slips away." The villain chuckled. "It must be very frustrating for you."

Something on another screen caught Destiny's attention. A video showed two training robots dragging a limp Batman and Green Arrow down the corridor.

"Delightful," said Doctor Destiny. He pressed a button, and the control room door slid open. The two robots marched in and dumped the unconscious heroes onto the floor. The robots left, and the door slid shut.

Doctor Destiny kneeled in front of the heroes. "I wonder what sweet dreams you two are having." He moved closer. "They won't be sweet for much longer." He leaned over Batman. "The doctor will see you now . . ."

Batman's eyes popped open, and he head-butted Destiny.

WHACK!

The villain cried out as he stumbled backward. Batman and Green Arrow sprang to their feet.

"Didn't see that one coming, did you?" Green Arrow asked.

Doctor Destiny shook his head and growled with anger. "You think you've won by getting close to me?"

Batman and Green Arrow spread out, moving to either side of the villain.

"Don't you remember, Batman?" asked Destiny. "The closer you get to me, the more powerful I become."

"Give it up, John," Batman ordered. "We don't have superpowers you can simply turn off with your mind."

"That's right," agreed Doctor Destiny. "But you're the World's Greatest Detective. . . . See if you can detect which one is the real me."

From Batman's point of view, the villain suddenly multiplied into a dozen Doctor Destinies. The Dark Knight fought madly as they all attacked at once. He punched, kicked, and threw Batarangs, but none of his blows landed. Instead, the multiple villains kept coming and coming.

Green Arrow watched as Batman punched and kicked nothing but thin air. He grunted as he frantically fought off invisible enemies.

Doctor Destiny chuckled and turned to Green Arrow. "You know, I hadn't even bothered controlling your mind before," he said. "But now I wonder how the World's Greatest Archer would feel if he missed me with every shot."

With lightning speed, Green Arrow pulled an arrow from his quiver and fired. Doctor Destiny didn't move a muscle as the arrow simply shot past him.

"That can't be," Green Arrow muttered. "I never miss."

He reached behind his back and retrieved another arrow. This time, he took his time to line up the shot. He released the arrow, but it missed again.

Doctor Destiny laughed as Green Arrow fired arrow after arrow. Each one zipped harmlessly past the villain.

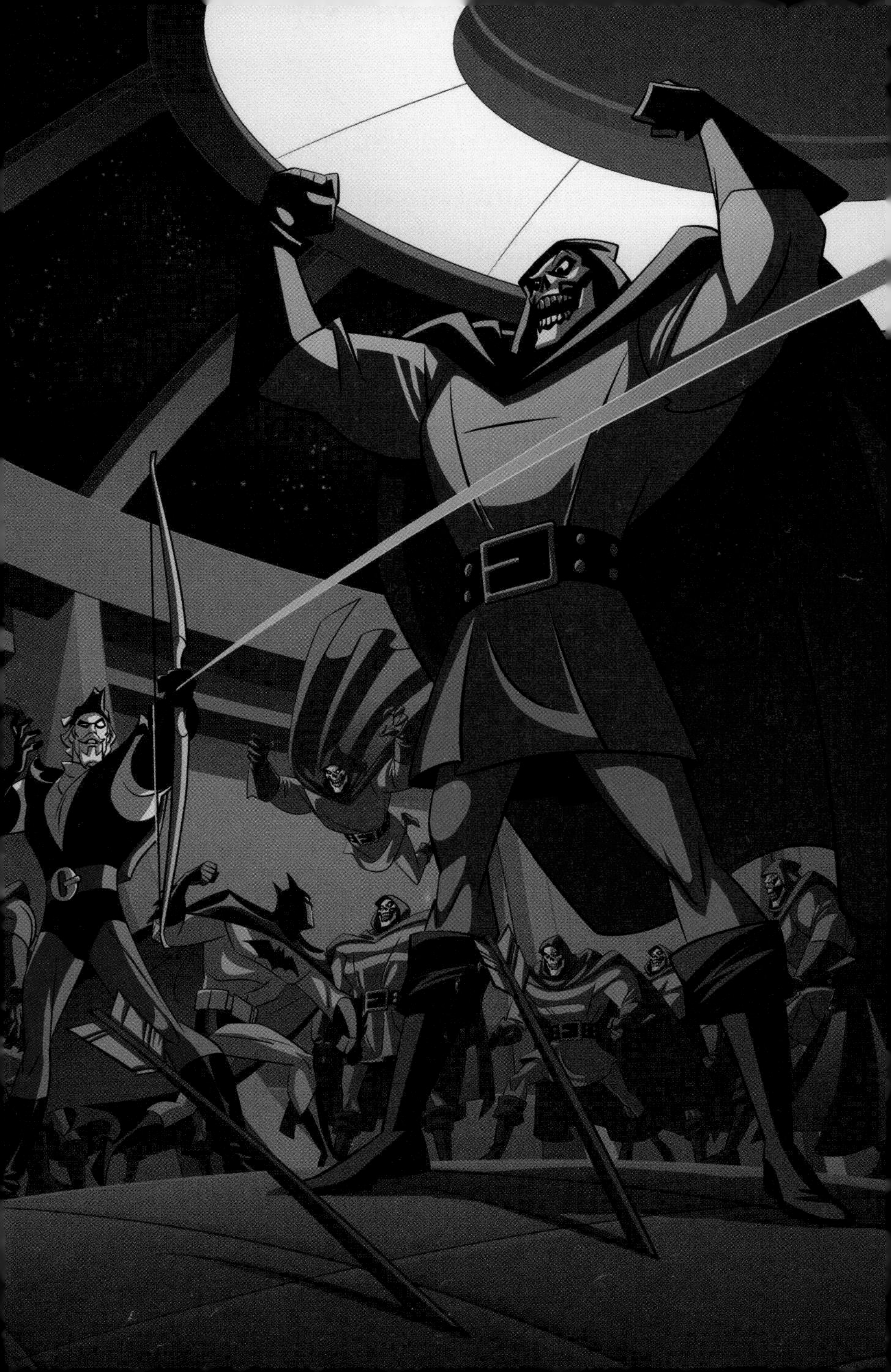

Green Arrow reached for his quiver and realized he had only one arrow left. He pulled it out, and his shoulders sank when he saw what it was. It was the arrow with the boxing glove on the end.

Destiny laughed. "You couldn't hit me with that one when I was Gray Hood."

The hero carefully loaded the arrow and took aim. Sweat formed on his brow as he concentrated with all his might. His arm trembled as he held the bowstring taut. Green Arrow held his breath and finally released the arrow.

Like the others, the shot zipped cleanly past Doctor Destiny.

"Missed again," Destiny taunted as the arrow flew by and bounced off the wall behind him. "And you're all out of arrows."

Green Arrow smiled. "I wasn't really aiming for you that time."

Destiny turned to see where the arrow had gone just in time to see it flying back toward him. *BAM!* It struck the villain square in the forehead.

Doctor Destiny fell back and slammed onto the ground, out cold. Once knocked out, his skull mask and costume faded away.

For Batman, all of his imaginary enemies vanished. Panting, he joined Green Arrow next to the man stretched out at his feet.

"Good job," Batman told Green Arrow.

WHOOSH!

The control center doors opened, and The Flash zipped inside. "We suddenly got our powers back and . . ." He leaned over the unconscious villain. "Hey . . . is that?"

"John Dee," Batman answered. "Also known as . . ."

"Doctor Destiny," Green Lantern finished as the rest of the heroes entered the room. "Man, that guy really has it out for the Justice League."

"He made us believe we were powerless?" Wonder Woman asked.

Batman nodded. "And he made us trust him completely."

"Well . . . ," Green Arrow rubbed his chin. "Not quite all of us."

"Good work," Superman said as he placed a hand on Green Arrow's shoulder. "We've always known it doesn't take superpowers to be a super hero."

"Yeah!" Green Arrow said. "Go, Team No-Superpowers!"

Green Arrow held out a fist to Batman. The Dark Knight didn't move. The hero held his fist for a second longer before finally dropping it.

"Okay, I get it. Batman doesn't fist bump," the Green Arrow said.

"Batman doesn't fist bump," the Dark Knight agreed.

Superman put a hand to his mouth to stop himself from laughing. The others weren't so successful. Even The Flash and Green Lantern chuckled as they hauled John Dee toward the holding cells.

Dr. Destiny

REAL NAME: John Dee

SPECIES: Metahuman

OCCUPATION: Professional Criminal

HEIGHT: 6 feet, 1 inch

WEIGHT: 171 lbs.

EYES: Black

HAIR: Brown

POWERS/ABILITIES:
Telepathy, mind control, and dream manipulation. He can also create dream worlds and has a vast medical knowledge.

BIOGRAPHY:

John Dee was a LexCorp employee who was caught by the Justice League while guarding smuggled weapons at a warehouse. While in prison, he was known as a good prisoner who got along well with the guards and prison warden. He also volunteered to be a test subject for the Materioptikon, an experimental extrasensory perception (ESP) machine. But deep inside, Dee wanted nothing more than to become strong enough to defeat the Justice League. Then, during a prison riot, he got his chance. He sneaked into a prison lab and turned the full power of the Materioptikon on himself. The machine gave him the power to control people's minds and twist their dreams. He became Dr. Destiny, and he soon escaped prison to wreak havoc on the world.

- Dr. Destiny's ability to control minds allows him to make people see things that aren't really there. For instance, his powers allow him to make people see him as his skeletal alter ego, rather than his true form as John Dee.

- Soon after escaping prison, Dr. Destiny broke into the dreams of The Flash, Superman, Green Lantern (John Stewart), and Hawkgirl. He trapped them inside their dreams and played off their deepest fears. Luckily, J'onn J'onzz, also known as the Martian Manhunter, used his own powers of telepathy to enter their dreams and help rescue them.

- Dr. Destiny has joined forces with several criminal organizations over the years. He has sided with Lex Luthor as a member of the Injustice Gang, and he has joined the ranks of the Legion of Doom. Destiny has even spent time in Gorilla Grodd's Secret Society.

BIOGRAPHIES

Author

Michael Anthony Steele has been in the entertainment industry for more than twenty-five years writing for television, movies, and video games. He has authored more than 110 books for exciting characters and brands including Batman, Superman, Green Lantern, Spider-Man, Shrek, Scooby-Doo, LEGO City, Garfield, Winx Club, Night at the Museum, and The Penguins of Madagascar. Mr. Steele lives on a ranch in Texas, but he enjoys meeting his readers when he visits schools and libraries all over the country.

Illustrator

Leonel Castellani has worked as a comic artist and illustrator for more than twenty years. Mostly known for his work on licensed art for companies such as Warner Bros., DC Comics, Disney, Marvel Entertainment, and Cartoon Network, Leonel has also built a career as a conceptual designer and storyboard artist for video games, movies, and TV. In addition to drawing, Leonel also likes to sculpt and paint. He currently lives in La Plata City, Argentina.

GLOSSARY

concentrate (KAHN-suhn-trayt)—to think clearly and to put your full attention on something

console (KON-sole)—a panel with dials and switches for controlling an electronic device

cosmic (KAHZ-mik)—having to do with outer space, the universe, or the heavens

destiny (DES-tih-nee)—a special purpose

grapnel (GRAP-nuhl)—a grappling hook connected to a rope that can be fired like a gun

imaginary (i-MAJ-uh-ner-ee)—existing in the mind and not in the real world

orbit (OR-bit)—to travel around an object in space

quiver (KWIV-ur)—a container for arrows

satellite (SAT-uh-lite)—a spacecraft that circles Earth

thug (THUHG)—a violent criminal

unconscious (uhn-KON-shuhss)—not awake; not able to see, feel, or think

virus (VYE-russ)—a germ that copies itself inside the body's cells

DISCUSSION QUESTIONS

1. Green Arrow isn't sure he should trust Gray Hood when he first meets him. But he decides to because he thinks Batman does. Why would Green Arrow trust Batman's judgment regarding Gray Hood over his own instincts?

2. Doctor Destiny's powers allow him to make others see reality the way he wants them to see it. What are some examples of him doing that in this story? How does he change the realities of the heroes with powers versus the heroes without powers?

3. Batman and Green Arrow have very different personalities. Batman is often very serious, while Green Arrow likes to joke around. Despite these differences, they still work well together as a team. Think of a time when you worked or played with someone who had a different personality than you. How did your differences affect your teamwork?

WRITING PROMPTS

1. Green Arrow uses a variety of trick arrows to fight criminals without harming them. If you could create your own trick arrow, what would it be? Write a paragraph that describes your arrow and explain how it would capture villains without harming them. Then draw a picture of it.

2. Doctor Destiny made up Gray Hood to trick the Justice League into thinking he was a super hero. Make up your own super hero and decide what powers or skills she or he will have. Then write a story in which your hero either helps or secretly hinders the Justice League.

3. The Flash and Green Lantern haul John Dee toward the Watchtower's holding cells at the end of the story. But what happens to the super-villain next? Does he go to prison or make a daring escape? Write a new chapter that continues Doctor Destiny's story.

LOOK FOR MORE

DC SUPER HERO ADVENTURES

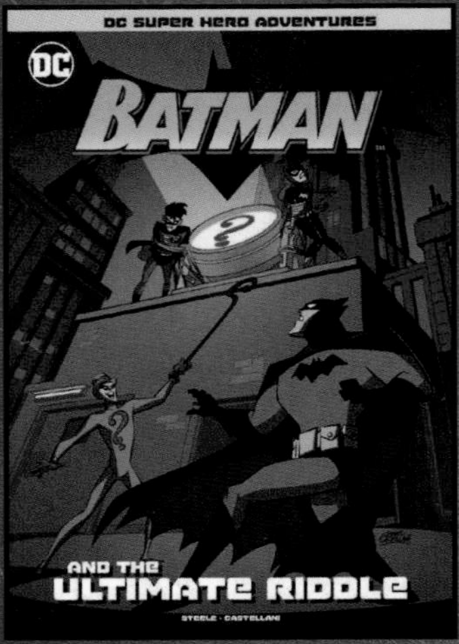
DC SUPER HERO ADVENTURES
DC
BATMAN
AND THE
ULTIMATE RIDDLE
STEELE · CASTELLANI

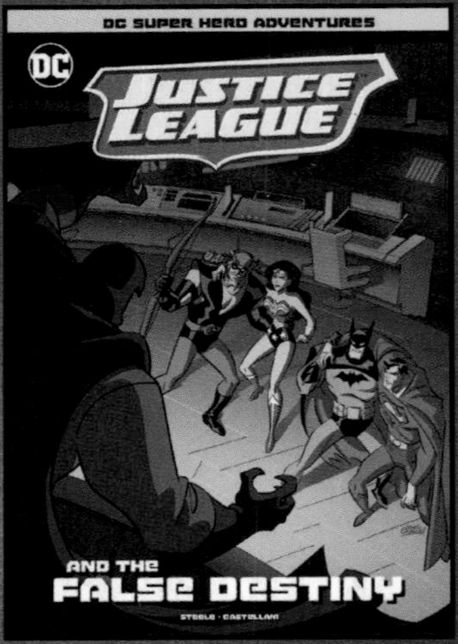
DC SUPER HERO ADVENTURES
DC
JUSTICE LEAGUE
AND THE
FALSE DESTINY

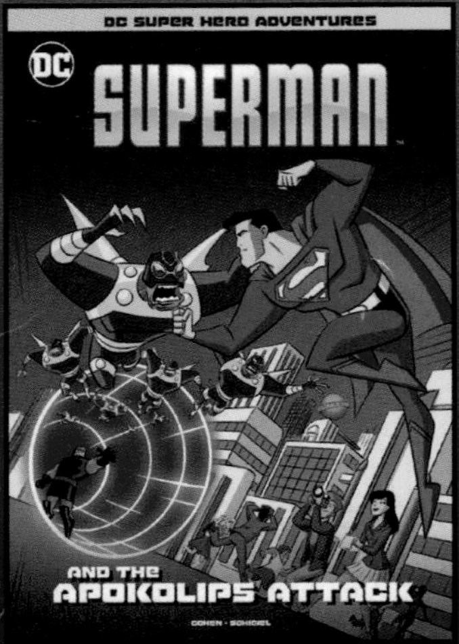
DC SUPER HERO ADVENTURES
DC
SUPERMAN
AND THE
APOKOLIPS ATTACK

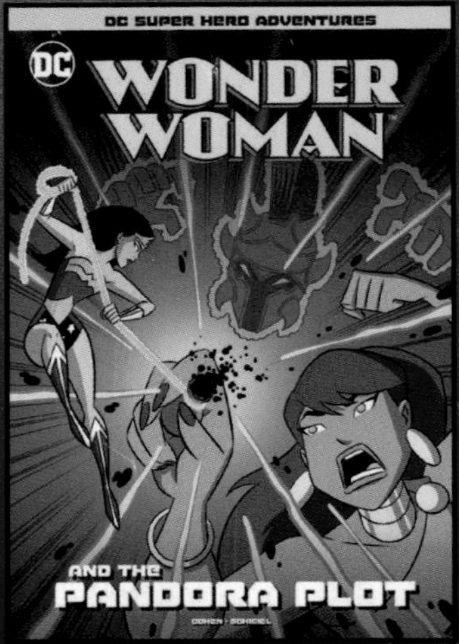
DC SUPER HERO ADVENTURES
DC
WONDER WOMAN
AND THE
PANDORA PLOT